JUST LIKE GRANDMA

by Kim Rogers

illustrated by Julie Flett

Heartdrum
An Imprint of HarperCollinsPublishers

On the steps of a house at the end of the street,
Becca watches
Grandma bead and bead
buckskin moccasins.

More than anything,
Becca wants to be
just like Grandma.

"Let me try," Becca says.
Grandma hands her thick thread and a thin needle.

Together they bead
until the sun dips below the tree line
and Grandpa calls them in for corn soup.

Out the window of a house at the end of the street,
Becca watches
Grandma dance barefoot near the garden,
spinning round and round and round,
like the most beautiful butterfly
Becca has ever seen.

More than anything,
Becca wants to be
just like Grandma.

She flitters out the back door and
stands near the garden barefoot, too.
"Let me try," she says.

Grandma shows Becca some dance moves
in the cool grass.

Together they flutter like the most beautiful butterflies
Grandpa has ever seen,
until the sun dips below the tree line
and he calls them in for fried chicken.

Inside Grandma's studio
Becca watches
Grandma paint and paint
a colorful sunrise.

More than anything,
Becca wants to be
just like Grandma.

Becca sits down next to
Grandma and her pretty palette.
"Let me try," she says.

Grandma shows her brushstrokes
on the textured canvas.

Together they paint the most spectacular sunrise
anyone has ever painted,
until the sun dips below the tree line
and Grandpa calls them in for pancakes for dinner.

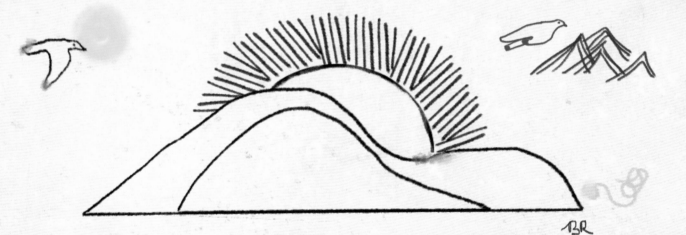

At the weekend powwow,
Becca watches
Grandma dance Fancy Shawl
with many other dancers
who are half her age.
She wins the grand prize!

More than anything,
Becca wants to be
just like Grandma.

When it's time for an intertribal,
Becca says, "Let me try."
Together she and Grandma dance
until the sun dips below the powwow arbor
and Grandpa calls them over for beans and fry bread.

Inside a house at the end of the street,
Grandma looks out the window
and watches Becca
all alone
with her ball.

Grandma sprints outside and stands next to Becca.

"Let me try," she says.
And Becca shows her
the plays she's been practicing
for basketball tryouts.

More than anything,
Grandma wants to be
just like Becca.

Together they shoot hoops
until the sun dips below the tree line
and Grandpa calls them in for to:kic and white bread.

At the school gym,
Grandma and Grandpa wait and wait in the hallway
during Becca's tryouts
so they don't make her nervous.

Becca dribbles, she shoots, she scores . . .

She makes the team!

Together they high-five
until the sun dips behind the gym
and Grandpa takes them out for pepperoni pizza.

They all laugh and eat and celebrate Becca's win.

On the steps of a house at the end of the street
Becca knows that
she is *just like Grandma.*

Beading,
dancing,
painting,
winning,

playing,
eating,
celebrating.
Spending time with her
and Grandpa, too.
Together.

And Grandma knows that
she is *just like Becca*.

A LETTER FROM CYNTHIA LEITICH SMITH

Dear Reader,

Do you have a role model—someone who inspires you to be more like them? Maybe your role model is a parent or teacher, an auntie or uncle, a neighbor, or a grandparent or other Elder.

Role models show us what's possible for ourselves . . . like Becca's grandma showed her it was possible to bead and dance and paint. Or maybe *you* are a role model to a sibling, cousin, or friend. You might even be a role model to a grown-up, like Becca is in inspiring Grandma to play basketball.

Elders can be loving, influential people in our lives. They are often caretakers, showing us how to nourish each other like Grandpa does for this family. Whether you have Elders in your day-to-day life or only through books like this one, I hope they inspire you in wonderful ways.

This picture book is published by Heartdrum, a Native-focused imprint of HarperCollins Children's Books that publishes stories about young Native heroes by Indigenous authors and illustrators. I'm delighted to include this book on the list because of the nurturing bond between Becca and her grandparents and because, when I was your age, my grandmothers—one stylish and strong-willed, the other homespun and good-humored—were among my life's greatest blessings.

Mvto,

Cynthia Leitich Smith

AUTHOR'S NOTE

Although this story is fiction, my grandmothers have always been a big part of my life. They are no longer with us, but I have fond memories of each of them: my great-grandmother, who was full of energy and went out dancing into her late seventies; my granny, who loved books just as much as I did; and my Wichita grandma, who I remember watching can vegetables and jams. I loved playing in her garden. Just like Becca's grandpa, my dad has always been the main cook for our family, taking good care of us. He still makes the best fried chicken in all the land!

In traditional Native American families, grandparents and Elders have always played a significant role in raising and educating children. They pass down cultural knowledge and kinship ties to ensure that they are continued on for future generations.

Families like Becca's are becoming more common. The number of children living in a grandparent's home has increased significantly over the past decade.

BEADWORK

Beadwork is one of the best-known art forms created by Native Americans. For thousands of years before the invasion of Europeans, Native people created their own beads using materials such as bone, shell, stone, and wood. They often used sand as an abrasive to shape the beads.

For centuries, the people of Native Nations throughout the continent traded beads with one another. They later traded with Europeans, Mexicans, Canadians, and US citizens. Glass and ceramic beads were one of the earliest goods Europeans traded with Native Americans.

Today, beadwork has become a way to symbolize and celebrate Native American heritage. At powwows, you will see extensive beadwork sewn onto the regalia of dancers. Regalia are not called costumes.

Many Natives proudly wear beadwork daily on earrings, bracelets, watches, hats, and other items. The art of beadwork is usually passed down from Elders in the family.

GLOSSARY

corn soup – Although this isn't a traditional Wichita dish from the Wichita tribe, which I am a member of, it's often served at intertribal powwows. (Intertribal powwows include more than one tribe.)

Fancy Shawl Dance – A fast-paced aerobic dance that is usually performed by younger dancers, although girls and women of any age can participate. The dancers resemble butterflies. The shawl is what gives the dance its name; it is fringed, colorful, and often beaded or appliquéd with various designs.

fry bread – A flatbread made of dough and fried in oil, shortening, or lard. Citizens and members of tribal Nations make it in a variety of ways. Even tribal members within the same tribe make it differently. It can be served as a side dish to accompany beans, as a taco shell, or as a dessert with honey or powdered sugar.

intertribal dance – A powwow dance where everyone who is invited by the emcee can dance with or without regalia.

palette – A board that artists use to mix and hold paint.

regalia – Outfits and accessories worn by Native dancers during traditional dances like powwows. Regalia is colorful and different depending on the dance and the personal style of the dancer. They are unique to every dancer and are often gifted to the dancers by Elders or other special people in the dancer's life.

to:kic – (pronounced doo-kits) A Wichita word meaning meat dish. It contains beef such as stew meat that is fried in grease; then flour is added to make a roux. Water is added to that to make a gravy. It's often eaten with fry bread, but my grandma served it with white sandwich bread.

In 2014, We Need Diverse Books (WNDB) began as a simple hashtag on Twitter. The social media campaign soon grew into a 501(c)(3) nonprofit with a team that spans the globe. WNDB is supported by a network of writers, illustrators, agents, editors, teachers, librarians, and book lovers, all united under the same goal— to create a world where every child can see themselves in the pages of a book. You can learn more about WNDB programs at www.diversebooks.org.

To Momma Mae (my great grandmother),
Granny, and Grandma. I miss you all.—K.R.

For Abigail, Annie, Josephine,
Ruby, and Shirley—J.F.

Heartdrum is an imprint of HarperCollins Publishers.

Library of Congress Control Number: 2022933344
ISBN 978-0-06-304924-6

The artist used pastels and pencil and digitally rendered the illustrations for this book.
Typography by Chelsea C. Donaldson • 22 23 24 25 26 RTLO 10 9 8 7 6 5 4 3 2 1 ❖ First Edition